WATER CYCLE ON WEATHER DAY

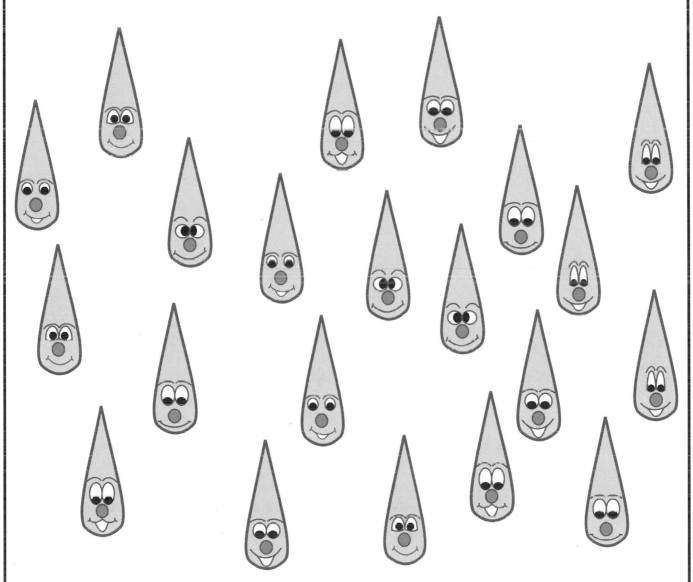

KlevaKids.com Inc

KlevaKids.com Inc

Presents

WATER CYCLE ON WEATHER DAY

This magical story introduces the concept of the water cycle. The sun evaporates water that turns to mist. The mist condenses as it rises into the atmosphere due to colder temperatures at higher elevations. Eventually, the mist concentrates enough to form water droplets that become rain.

The above statements are purely informational. The purpose of the book is not to teach, but to expose concepts. Read the book to a child and just allow the story to be enjoyed.

It always starts ordinary,

the magical Weather Day.

Weather elements come to life.

They take turns for water cycle play.

The sun awakens,

smiling so warmly,

radiating rays,

shining so brightly.

The ocean has a laugh

that is like a mighty roar.

It creates a lot of ripples,

that turn to waves galore.

The sun shines so warmly,

radiating heat and light.

The waves start to evaporate

and lose a bit of height.

Now the waves get smaller

as mist rises.

If this stuff continues,

there might be surprises.

Now the mist rises high,

it forms a little puff.

What is this?

This is unusual stuff.

The puff got bigger

and now we know

it was a cloud

that formed so slow.

More mist rose

and the cloud then grew.

It blocked out the sun

that we once knew.

The cloud got dark,

very dark you see.

Whatever, whatever

could this be?

Drips formed on the cloud,

on the bottom, not the top.

There were many, many drips,

not just one rain drop.

Alas, many rain drops fell

with awesome power.

This was a beautiful,

wonderous rain shower.

As the rain drops fell,

the cloud became smaller.

Everything was returning

to its original order.

The sun was visible again

with a smile so bright.

The waves were returning

to their original height.

Sunshine turns water to mist rising above all.

Mist makes clouds for rain drops to fall.

Alas, it was the end of magical Weather Day

and joyous water cycle play.

THE END